This book belongs to:

~~THE~~

~~MOON~~ BUGS

_____

SPACE BLASTERS
SUZIE AND THE MOON BUGS

First published in Great Britain in 2023 by Farshore
An imprint of HarperCollins*Publishers*
1 London Bridge Street, London SE1 9GF

farshore.co.uk

HarperCollins*Publishers*,
Macken House, 39/40 Mayor Street Upper, Dublin 1, D01 C9W8, Ireland

Text copyright © Katie and Kevin Tsang 2023
Illustration copyright © Amy Nguyen 2023

The moral rights of the authors and illustrator have been asserted

ISBN 978 0 7555 0028 4

Printed and bound in the UK using 100% renewable electricity at
CPI Group (UK) Ltd

1

A CIP catalogue record for this title is available from the British Library.

KATIE & KEVIN TSANG
ILLUSTRATED BY AMY NGUYEN

SPACE BLASTERS
SUZIE AND THE MOON BUGS

Farshore

**For Mira and Evie,
our little explorers.**

CONTENTS

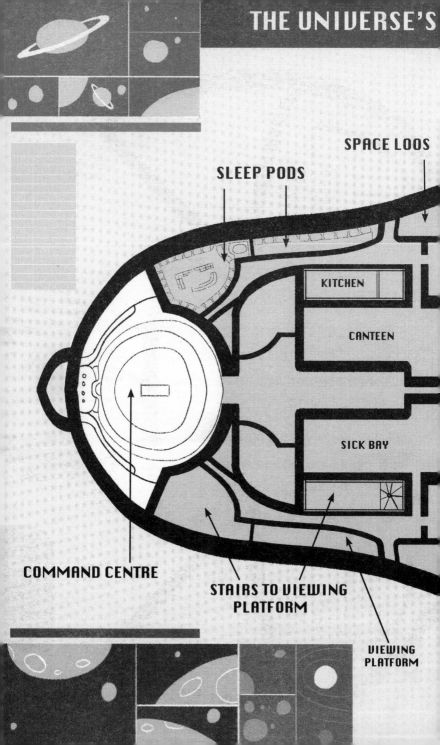

SPACE LOOS

SLEEP PODS

KITCHEN

CANTEEN

SICK BAY

COMMAND CENTRE

STAIRS TO VIEWING
PLATFORM

VIEWING
PLATFORM

BEST SPACECRAFT (TUBS)

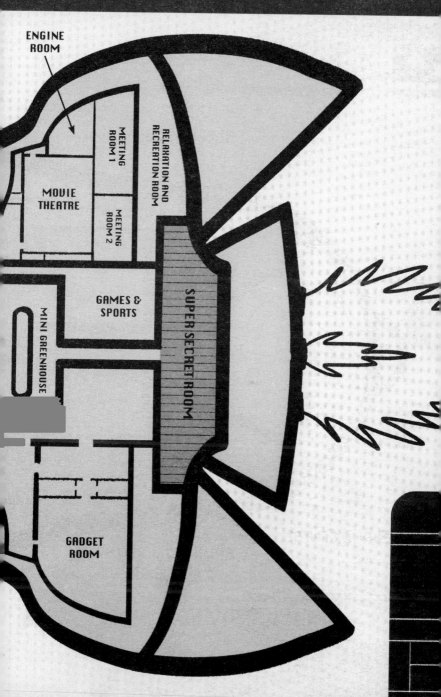

ENGINE ROOM

MEETING ROOM 1

RELAXATION AND RECREATION ROOM

MOVIE THEATRE

MEETING ROOM 2

GAMES & SPORTS

SUPER SECRET ROOM

MINI GREENHOUSE

GADGET ROOM

CHAPTER 1

TOTAL
CHAOS

Have you ever found yourself in a situation that is COMPLETELY out of control? One moment, everything is fine, and the next moment, everything is CHAOS?

This is something that frequently happens to me.

But I'd NEVER had things spiral out of control like they did when I joined the Space Blasters crew. And that includes the time I invented a dumpling maker that exploded all over the kitchen and splattered in my older sister's face.

OK, that was pretty bad – but little did I know that things were about to get way more out of control.

Because I definitely wasn't expecting to get sucked into my favourite TV show, *Space Blasters*, become part of the crew, and help them save the universe.

In space, *anything* can happen. And no matter how prepared you think you are, you are bound to be surprised.

I should probably introduce myself. I'm Suzie Wen. I'm an inventor, dumpling enthusiast and brand-new member of the Space Blasters crew.

When I'm not in space helping save the universe, I live at home with my mum, dad, older sister Lizzie and older brother David. You might think that living with four people

means I always have someone to talk to or hang out with, but everyone in my family is *always* busy. My parents work a lot, David spends all his time practising his drums in the garage, and Lizzie is always out with her friends. They are both older than me and NEVER let me forget that I'm the baby. And apparently they have no time for me either.

We used to see my grandparents, my gung-gung and my po-po, all the time, but then they moved to the seaside.

If all that wasn't bad enough, my best friend Bonnie also moved away. All the way to New York City!

Leaving me stuck at home for the entire summer with nobody to spend time with.

Until something INCREDIBLE happened. I was trying to invent a **Super 3-D TV Gizmo** so I could feel like I was really in my favourite shows, so at least I'd have some company, but then something went very wrong, or very right, and instead of making *Space Blasters* 3-D . . . I found myself zapped into the world of the show itself!

Which is how I ended up here. In *Space Blasters*. Part of the crew, flying TUBS (that

4

stands for The Universe's Best Spacecraft),
along with Captain Jane, Spaceman Jack
and the alien Five-Eyed Frank.

I had already helped them save the universe once, when we tracked down the dream-eater alien and convinced it to stop stealing moons and putting entire planets to sleep. And just when I thought my life couldn't get any stranger, we crash-landed on the most mysterious planet imaginable!

I knew it was up to me and the crew to figure out what was wrong – and ultimately to save the universe once more!

CHAPTER 2

EMERGENCY ALERT

Before the crash landing, there was an emergency alert.

I knew it was an emergency alert because TUBS kept repeating in its robotic voice:

'ALERT! ALERT! ALERT! EMERGENCY ALERT! ALL SYSTEMS FAILING! EMERGENCY ALERT!' while red and blue lights flashed overhead.

'Everyone! Strap yourself in your space chairs!' cried Captain Jane. 'Buckle up! Looks like we are going to have to make an emergency landing.'

We had been on our way to respond to a distress signal from a planet on the other side of the galaxy, but there was no way we could make it now. Not with TUBS having a system malfunction. That planet would have to wait until TUBS was working properly again.

I gulped and tightened my seat belt. 'On it!' I knew how important it was to listen to Captain Jane, especially in a moment like this.

'I hate emergency landings!' shrieked Five-Eyed Frank, all of his eyes frantically darting around.

'Not much of a fan of them myself,' said Spaceman Jack, looking a bit green. And he was human, like me, so was never really supposed to look green.

I have to specify that I'm human because not everyone you meet in space is. When I first joined the crew, Five-Eyed Frank made me prove that I was human. I did it by telling a knock-knock joke.

TUBS kept repeating warnings as the entire spaceship shuddered and shook, like the entire thing could fall apart at any moment! **'ALERT! ALERT! ALL SYSTEMS FAILING - LAND IMMEDIATELY! LAND IMMEDIATELY!'**

'DO SOMETHING, CAPTAIN JANE!'
screeched Frank.

'I AM DOING SOMETHING!' she yelled
back. It was the first time I'd ever heard
Captain Jane shout, and that was when I
knew things must be bad. She seemed to
realise she was yelling because she took a
long, deep breath. When she spoke again,
her voice was calmer. 'I am landing on the
nearest planet.'

'BUT WE DON'T KNOW WHAT PLANET
THAT IS!' Frank was still yelling, but he
yelled whenever he was anxious, so it wasn't
alarming. 'WHAT IF IT IS DANGEROUS!'

'It can't be more dangerous than staying
in a spaceship that has all systems failing,'
I pointed out.

Frank glared at me with all five of his
eyes and stuck his tongue out. 'Now you

are acting like a know-it-all knowledge worm.'

'What's a knowledge worm again?' I said.

'Exactly what it sounds like. A worm from Planet Zorg that KNOWS IT ALL.'

I sighed. Frank and I were . . . *tentative* friends. **I** wanted to be his friend, but **he** was still extremely suspicious of **me**. Even after we had worked together – not only to save the entire universe, but also rescue Spaceman Jack and Captain Jane from getting tangled up in Planet Knot forever – and I had officially become a member of the crew, he didn't totally trust me.

I knew I still had to prove myself to him.

And this crash landing could be the perfect chance!

Part of me knew I should be scared. After all, I was on a spaceship about to make

an emergency crash landing. But instead
of focusing on that, I focused on what I
could control. Like my breathing. I took a
long breath in, and then released it. In and
out, in and out. This was a trick my po-po
(that is what I call my grandma) taught me
when I felt like I was in a situation that was
spiralling out of control.

'Why are you huffing and puffing over
there?' said Five-Eyed Frank.

'I'm focusing on my breathing,' I said.
'To stay calm.' I gave him an encouraging
smile. 'You should try it.'

'HOW CAN ANYONE BE CALM WHEN
WE ARE ABOUT TO CRASH-LAND ON A
MYSTERY PLANET?'

So much for focusing on our breathing.

Three-Headed Tommy, Spaceman Jack's
flying lizard, chirped in alarm next to my

ear. If Tommy was worried, we really were in trouble! I'd never seen the flying lizard get anxious.

'We are going to be OK, right?' I asked. My voice came out a lot squeakier than I was expecting.

'Of course we will,' said Captain Jane as she pulled back hard on one of the space controllers. 'Everybody, HOLD ON!'

I was flung back in my seat as we sped towards the mystery planet. My stomach was doing somersaults.

'I feel a little . . .' I started to say but

Spaceman Jack held his hand up.

'Don't even say it! Don't say the S word!' he said, eyes wide with panic.

'Sick?' As soon as the word left my mouth, Spaceman Jack turned even MORE green, opened his mouth, and threw up all over his space boots.

CHAPTER 3

STUCK SEAT BELTS AND STRANGE SOUNDS

'Whoops,' I said, trying not to stare at the puddle of vomit sloshing around the floor of the spaceship. 'Sorry.'

'He did tell you not to say it,' said Five-Eyed Frank. '*I* never say the S word in front of Spaceman Jack.'

I felt my cheeks flame. 'I really am sorry.'

'It's fine,' said Spaceman Jack, wiping his mouth with the back of his hand. 'Not your fault.'

'Well, if she hadn't said it,' pointed out

Five-Eyed Frank.

'Frank, my five-eyed friend, I'll remind you that you said the S word to me on that mission to Planet Florp, remember? I threw up in our space pod,' said Jack.

'Oh, I do remember that,' said Five-Eyed Frank with a grimace. 'It got everywhere.'

I felt my stomach do another flip. 'Could we maybe stop talking about it? I think I'm starting to understand why even saying the word could make you feel a bit . . .'

'DON'T SAY IT AGAIN!' cried Five-Eyed Frank.

'I won't!' I really hoped we were going to land soon. TUBS was still shaking so hard I thought it might explode before we even made it to the mystery planet!

I leaned my head against the headrest, trying to stay calm. As I did, the strangest

thing happened. I thought I heard
giggling inside the walls.

'TUBS?' I said, knocking gently on
the wall. 'Is that you laughing?'

But if TUBS heard me, it didn't
reply. It kept blaring: **'EMERGENCY
ALERT! EMERGENCY ALERT! LAND
IMMEDIATELY!'**

'I'm trying
my best!' said
Captain Jane.
'I just hope this
is a friendly
planet that won't
mind us crash-
landing.'

I gulped.
I hadn't even
thought of that!

So far most of the planets we visited had been friendly, even Planet Knot, which was populated by tangles. Tangles, I now knew, were aliens that you could literally get tangled up in. The more anxious they became, the more knotty things got.

But they hadn't been unfriendly when we visited them while tracking down the missing moons.

Crash-landing on a mystery planet was scary enough. The idea of crash-landing on a planet with hostile aliens was terrifying!

'Can't we try to land on a friendly planet?' I called out.

'No can do,' said Spaceman Jack. 'I've never heard TUBS break down like this. We need to land, and we need to land fast.'

'Like I said, I'm doing my best,' replied Captain Jane in a strained voice. 'I'll land this ship if it is the last thing I do.'

'That isn't as reassuring as you think it is,' said Spaceman Jack.

'I agree,' I added. 'I really, really hope it isn't the last thing you do.'

TUBS was rattling so much now that I was worried that pieces were going to start flying off before we landed. But then

with a **WHOOSH** that I felt all the way in my bones, we shot through the planet's atmosphere, and then there was an enormous **THUMP**.

We had landed.

19

I clapped my hands and cheered. But instead of celebrating her successful landing, Captain Jane sprang into action.

'We have to get off the ship before TUBS fully shuts down,' said Captain Jane, throwing my space helmet at me. 'I'll grab our emergency space packs and meet you all at the exit chute.'

I caught my space helmet and jammed it on my head. My heart was beating so hard inside my chest I practically expected it to burst out of my body.

'Jumpin' Jupiter, my seat belt is stuck!' said Spaceman Jack. 'TUBS! Release my seat belt!'

'TUBS IS SHUTTING DOWN! TUBS IS SHUTTING DOWN!' repeated the spaceship's robotic voice.

I quickly pressed down on my own seat-belt release button, let out a huge sigh of relief when it worked, and then scrambled out of my seat. But as I did, I heard it again.

FUN FACT!

The seat-belt was invented by an engineer called Nils Bohlin.

That strange giggling in the walls.

'TUBS?' I said, knocking gently. 'Is that you?' There was no reply. I frowned. Something VERY strange was going on.

'I'm trapped!' shouted Spaceman Jack, louder and more panicked now. 'Someone get me out of this thing!' I'd never seen him this agitated when watching the show.

'Don't worry, Spaceman Jack!' cried Five-Eyed Frank, already out of his seat. 'I'll help you! Just stay still!' To my complete shock, his fingertip lit up and a LASER shot out. It sliced through the seat belt, freeing

Spaceman Jack.

'Well done, Frank,' said Spaceman Jack. 'You didn't even singe my spacesuit!'

'WHOA!' I burst out. 'How did you do that?'

Five-Eyed Frank rolled all of his eyes. 'I'm an alien, remember? I have all sorts of tricks you don't know about.'

I was so impressed I didn't even care that he was being rude. 'Well, that was AWESOME.' I held up my hand. 'Palm five!'

The corner of Five-Eyed Frank's mouth twitched up, and then he smacked his hand against mine. 'Palm five!'

Palm five was what Five-Eyed Frank called a 'high five'. And I have to admit, it was a more accurate term.

'Come on, you two. We need to get off this ship before it does anything else

23

strange,' said Spaceman Jack. 'Something is very wrong.' And again, I could have sworn I heard the strange giggles echoing in the ship.

'Can anyone else hear that?' I said, but Five-Eyed Frank and Spaceman Jack were already hurrying towards the exit chute. So, with one more curious look around me, I ran after them.

CHAPTER 4

MYSTERY PLANET

Captain Jane, Spaceman Jack, Five-Eyed Frank and Tommy the three-headed lizard were waiting for me.

'Tommy is coming too?' I said, petting the lizard on his middle head.

'Everyone is coming,' said Captain Jane firmly. 'TUBS is acting so strange, it isn't safe to leave anyone on the ship. I don't want to risk anyone getting trapped on board. And that includes Tommy.'

Tommy chirped in gratitude.

'I'll be the last one off, just to make sure I've shut everything down. And then we'll hopefully figure out what is wrong with TUBS, repair it and be back on our flight course,' said Captain Jane.

'I'll go first,' announced Spaceman Jack. 'To secure our perimeter and check for any immediate danger. Frank and Suzie can go between us. That is the safest way.'

'I really don't want to leave the ship,' wailed Five-Eyed Frank. 'Especially because this is a MYSTERY PLANET.'

I felt a pang of sympathy for him. I knew he didn't like going into the unknown.

I gave him what I hoped was an encouraging smile. 'Don't worry, we'll all be together!' I said confidently.

It didn't have the comforting effect I was hoping for. Five-Eyed Frank scowled back at me. 'You don't have any skills! How will you help us?'

I felt my lips begin to quiver and my smile quickly disappeared. I gulped, and really hoped I wouldn't start to cry. The only thing worse than being a crew member who didn't have any skills, was one who was also a crybaby.

'Frank!' Captain Jane said sternly. 'That isn't nice or true. Suzie has lots of skills. Remember how well you two worked together to track down the dream-eating alien?'

Frank sighed dramatically. 'I suppose you are right,' he said. Then he rolled all of his eyes. 'Pleaseacceptmyapology.' His words came out all in one.

'What was that?' said Captain Jane. 'I couldn't hear you.'

'I said Please. Accept. My. Apology,' Frank said, this time over-enunciating each word. He sighed again. 'And you do have skills. I'm sorry. I get grumpy when I get nervous. And I'm VERY NERVOUS right now.'

'Frank, my friend, you are always nervous,' said Spaceman Jack with a booming laugh. Then he winked at me and dropped his voice to a whisper. 'That explains why he is always grumpy.'

'I heard that,' grumbled Frank, but he was smiling now. 'I really am sorry, Suzie. I forgot that even though you are a small human with zero space experience, you still are a useful member of the crew.' He held his hand out. 'Palm five?'

I smiled back at him. 'Apology accepted. Palm five!'

'Now that that's settled, shall we go

explore this mystery planet and then try
to fix TUBS?' said Captain Jane.

I nodded. 'Absolutely! For the universe!'
I shot my hand up into the air, doing the
Space Blasters, salute.

The others laughed. 'For the universe!'

I didn't know what to expect when I
zoomed down the exit chute towards this
new mystery planet.

I was ready for anything.

But nothing had prepared me for what
was waiting for us.

I tried to land feet first, the way I'd seen
Spaceman Jack and Captain Jane do, but
I lost my balance and fell on my bum. As
I hopped up, I gasped.

We had crash-landed in a rainbow jungle!

Everywhere I looked there were
shimmering, shiny colours. Huge leaves
of all shades flapped over me and long,
wavy purple grass lay beneath my feet.
Vines covered in sparkling pink and yellow
flowers tumbled down from the trees.

And everything was so BRIGHT! It was
like the colours were turned up to the max.

Then I heard a familiar voice next to me.
'All clear!'

It was Spaceman Jack, who was using
his detector beam to scan the area around
us. I knew the detector beam was seeking
life forms.

Five-Eyed Frank was hiding

behind Spaceman Jack,

cautiously peering out

at the vibrant world we

had found ourselves

in. Three-Headed

Tommy, who must

have come down with

Spaceman Jack, was

sitting on Spaceman

Jack's shoulder.

There was a whoosh and then Captain Jane appeared. 'Any idea where we are?' she asked.

'My scanner isn't picking up anything familiar,' said Spaceman Jack. 'But the atmosphere here is similar to Earth, so we can take off our helmets.' He pressed a button on his scanner again and pointed it at the grass and vines in front of us. 'My scanner recognises that these are plant forms with no sign of poison or venom, but it doesn't know what they are, so we should be wary.'

'They are beautiful,' I said.

'The important thing is we stay together,' said Captain Jane – but as she spoke, the ground beneath us began to shake and the wavy purple grass shot up like a wall with me and Five-Eyed Frank on one side and Captain Jane and Spaceman Jack on the other.

CHAPTER 5

LOST

Five-Eyed Frank and I looked at each other.
Then we both began yelling as loud as we
could.

But more and more grass kept shooting
up towards the sky. In moments, not
only could we not see Spaceman Jack
and Captain Jane any longer, we couldn't
even see TUBS! And then I realised the
ground was ROLLING beneath us, like a
roller coaster, and moving us further away
from where we had started. The more the
ground rolled, the taller the purple grass

grew, and the more confused I became about where we were.

Right as the ground pitched beneath us, Five-Eyed Frank did something I thought he would never do. He grabbed my hand and held on for dear life.

'We can't lose each other!' he cried, all of his eyes wider than I'd ever seen them.

'CAPTAIN JANE! SPACEMAN JACK!' I shouted, hoping they would hear us. But the only sound was the whoosh of the purple grass growing taller and taller all around us.

Finally, the ground stopped shifting, and everything was still.

Five-Eyed Frank and I clutched each other's hands, and waited for a moment to see what would happen next.

Nothing.

'Try the intercom,' Frank finally said.

'The what?'

Frank huffed. 'The intercom! On your spacesuit.'

'My spacesuit has an intercom?'

'Of course it does! There, on your wrist.'

I carefully pressed the intercom. 'Captain Jane! I repeat, Captain Jane!' I said. 'This is Suzie and Frank, do you copy?'

I had heard someone on a different TV

show say that once, and I wasn't exactly sure what it meant, but it sounded official.

My intercom buzzed with static.

'Exploding moons,' muttered Frank. 'No luck.' Then he brightened. 'I know! We will send up a flare so they know where we are!'

'What is a flare?'

Frank sighed deeply. 'I keep forgetting how much you don't know.'

'There is no shame in not knowing anything,' I said stubbornly. 'Only a chance to learn something new!'

'Well, you have a LOT of chances to learn things,' Frank said quietly, but not so quietly that I didn't hear him.

'Focus, Frank!' I said.

'Right, right,' he said. 'A flare is a type of signal, usually made of fire or light, to show where we are.'

I frowned. 'But if Spaceman Jack and Captain Jane are also lost in this long, wavy grass, how will they see our flare?'

'Do you have any better ideas?' Frank snapped.

I shrugged. 'OK. Send up the flare!'

Frank waggled his fingers. Just like when he had sliced open Spaceman Jack's seat belt, his fingertips lit up with small green

laser beams. He held his hand up and the
lasers shot into the air.

'Whoa,' I said.

Frank nodded. 'I know,' he said seriously.
'I am awesome.'

The laser flares soared higher and higher
and then exploded into fireworks far above
our head.

'Now what?' I asked.

'We wait for them to find us,' said Frank, sitting down and crossing his legs. 'I am staying RIGHT HERE.'

'But what if they don't see the flares?'

'Of course they will see them!' Frank insisted. 'And they will follow them and find us!'

I swallowed. 'And until then . . . we are lost?'

'We are not lost. We are waiting to be found. Different things entirely,' said Frank with his eyes closed. 'Now I'm going to take a nap.'

'A NAP?' I squeaked. 'But what if another creature on this planet finds us?'

'You stay awake,' Frank ordered. 'And deal with any of these mystery creatures.'

'DEAL WITH THEM HOW? I DON'T HAVE

LASER FINGERS!' I didn't realise I was shouting until the words were out of my mouth.

Frank sighed again. 'That is why I said you don't have any skills.'

I frowned at him. 'I have *some* skills! I just don't have laser finger!'

'Well, use those skills to deal with anything that finds us,' said Frank. And he closed his eyes and went to sleep.

I paced around him in a circle, trying to look in every direction. Really, Frank should have been the one on alert. He had five eyes and I only had two. He could see way more than I could!

And all I saw was the tall, wavy grass.

FUN FACT!

LASER is actually an acronym for 'Light Amplification by Stimulated Emission of Radiation'.

It was rippling in a breeze, and every time it rustled, it made me jump.

'Just the wind, just the wind,' I told myself.

Overhead, our flare still glowed in the sky. Alerting Spaceman Jack and Captain Jane to where we were.

A terrible thought occurred to me.

The flare wouldn't just alert Spaceman Jack and Captain Jane. It would alert any other curious life forms that might be on this mystery planet.

Right as I was having that thought, the tall grass rustled again. But this time it was a different kind of rustle. One that sounded distinctly like footsteps.

I gulped and poked Frank. 'Frank, WAKE UP.'

Frank's eyes immediately flew open.

'There's something there,' I whispered.

42

'In the grass.'

Frank leaped to his feet and peered around. His fingertips began to glow as his lasers warmed up.

'We should go back-to-back,' he said. 'I learned that from Spaceman Jack. That way nothing can sneak up on us.'

So we went back-to-back and stood, waiting for whatever was in the grass.

Then I saw a familiar swoop of blonde hair and I breathed a huge sigh of relief.

'It's Spaceman Jack!' I cried, and I took off towards the figure.

'No! Spaceman Jack is over there!' said Five-Eyed Frank.

I stopped, looked over my shoulder and gasped. There was ANOTHER Spaceman Jack walking right towards us.

CHAPTER 6

TOO MANY SUZIES

I narrowed my eyes. 'Which one do you think is the real Spaceman Jack?'

'I don't know yet,' said Five-Eyed Frank. 'But I intend to find out urgently.'

Frank cupped his hands and brought them to his mouth before letting out a burst of howls that sounded exactly like a howler monkey I had once seen at a zoo.

What was he doing? The last thing we needed was to draw so much attention to ourselves.

'Frank, this is no time to be monkeying around!' I tugged at Frank's arm but he just howled louder.

Both Spaceman Jacks stopped and looked at Frank. The closer Spaceman Jack gave me a toothy smile that didn't quite reach his eyes.

'It's definitely not that one giving us the weird smile,' I said.

Frank frowned. 'How peculiar. Neither of them returned my emergency alert.'

I stared blankly at him.

Frank let out a huff. 'Obviously Spaceman Jack and I, like all reasonably prepared intergalactic explorers, have an agreed emergency alert in case of emergencies, which is precisely the situation we find ourselves in.'

'That is sensible,' I said, nodding. 'But why a monkey howl?'

'Gertie – you remember us telling you about her, the monkey who used to be on our crew before she retired to a tropical planet in the distant Zadar galaxy?' Frank said, speaking very quickly as more and more Spaceman Jacks approached us. 'She taught us the monkey howl. Very useful.' He did the howl again.

The Spaceman Jacks didn't respond.

'They are definitely not the real Spaceman Jack,' muttered Frank.

'Unless . . .' An idea had just struck me. 'Do you think one of these IS the real Spaceman Jack and something's wrong with him?' I paused. 'Like maybe he's been brainwashed or something?'

'Unlikely,' said Five-Eyed Frank.

Another poof of blonde hair popped up from the tall, purple grass. Then another, and another. Soon there were so many Spaceman Jacks that there was more yellow than purple in front of us.

Five-Eyed Frank's eyes darted all around. 'They seem to be *multiplying* somehow.'

I brought my hands to my head and closed my eyes to concentrate. Whenever there is a problem I can't figure out, I can't help but try to think of the answer. 'I know!' I said. 'Maybe Spaceman Jack is really a robot and he is part of a huge robot clan with other robots that look just like him?'

'Don't be ridiculous, Suzie,' said Five-Eyed Frank as he brought his hands back to his mouth and howled at the sea of Spaceman Jacks.

Before I could say anything else, something tapped me on the shoulder. I turned and saw . . . *me*. I was looking directly into the eyes of something that looked exactly like me.

I yelped and scuttled backwards. 'FRANK! SOMETHING WEIRD IS GOING ON.'

Five-Eyed Frank turned and studied both of us. 'Well, this is an interesting development. Which one of you is the real Suzie?'

'Me!' I cried. 'You have to trust me!'

'Hmmm,' said Five-Eyed Frank.
'Unfortunately we have not yet come up
with an agreed signal between the two of
us to prove we are who we say we are. You
see, this is why you need one.'

I desperately began to do the same howl
he had done when trying to find the real
Spaceman Jack.

'What are you doing?' said Five-Eyed
Frank, wrinkling his face in confusion. 'Stop
making that awful racket!'

'The sound! To prove who I am!'

Frank rolled his middle eye. 'We
obviously do not make the same sound.
That is too easy to replicate! Spaceman
Jack has his own secret response that is
different to mine. And anyway, if you are
trying to make my alert, you are doing it
wrong.' He began to howl again. 'It goes
like this – OOOH-OOH-OOOOOOOOOH!
Completely different.'

'OK, OK. But at least you know it is me,
right?' I said.

'Hmmm,' said Five-Eyed Frank. He turned
to the other Suzie. 'What do YOU have to
say for yourself?'

The other Suzie smiled at both of us and

belched. '*Blorp, blorp.'*

I let out a sigh of relief. At least it wasn't trying to talk like me.

'*Blorp, blorp, blorp*,' the other Suzie continued.

'Ah,' said Five-Eyed Frank. 'That proves it.'

Just then we heard a thankfully familiar voice. 'FRANK! SUZIE? Where are you?'

The *real* Spaceman Jack bounded through the sea of other Spaceman Jacks. Captain Jane was running by his side.

Spaceman Jack cupped his hands around his mouth and cawed like a crow. '*CAW, CAW, CAW!'*

All of Five-Eyed Frank's eyes lit up and he began howling like a monkey again. As Spaceman Jack reached us, Five-Eyed Frank held out an open hand. 'It is the real you!' he said happily. 'Palm five!'

Spaceman Jack grinned at Frank and gave him a palm five.

'I sure am glad to see you two,' said Spaceman Jack. 'Or should I say . . . you six.'

I looked behind me and gasped. There was *another* Suzie, and two new Franks! What was this place? Trying to figure it out was making my brain hurt. 'Do you know what is going on?'

Spaceman Jack flashed me a twinkling smile. 'Have you ever seen so many good-looking and charming spacemen all in one place?'

Captain Jane, or at least someone who looked like Captain Jane, shook her head and laughed. 'Don't mind him, Suzie. He's just happy to see himself.' She walked over to a different Spaceman Jack standing a few metres away and assessed him. He stuck out his tongue at her and cocked his head to the side.

'These are replicators,' explained Captain Jane. 'They've got a special ability to morph into any shape they please. But they need a form to replicate. And these ones have obviously chosen to replicate us.'

'How do we make them stop?' I said. Seeing so many versions of myself was making me feel funny.

'Like this.' Captain Jane balled her hand into a fist and bonked the fake Spaceman Jack on the top of the head three times.

The Spaceman Jack smiled as he morphed into what looked like a *huge* gecko that stood on two legs. It was twice as tall as me. The gecko creature stuck out its tongue and licked its eye, before turning

back into an exact replica of Spaceman Jack. It gave me a crooked smile. '*Blorp, blorp.*'

CHAPTER 7

THREE NOSES ARE
BETTER THAN NONE

'REPLICATORS! OF COURSE!' cried Five-
Eyed Frank. 'I should have known right
away!' He smacked his hand against his
forehead, nearly poking himself in one of
his eyes. 'And if we are seeing this many
replicators, it means only ONE THING.'

He stared at me, as if waiting for me to
reply.

'Erm, what does it mean?' I said, still trying
to get my head round the idea of creatures
that could turn into other creatures.

'Isn't it obvious?' said Five-Eyed Frank, bouncing with impatience.

'Not to me,' I admitted, frowning. The other Suzie in front of me frowned back.

'WE ARE ON PLANET ZORG!' Five-Eyed Frank crowed triumphantly.

'Of course!' said Spaceman Jack, also smacking his hand on his forehead.

'Ah, of course,' I said, still totally confused about what was happening. The other Suzie stopped frowning and stuck its tongue out at me. Without thinking, I stuck *my* tongue out back. 'So how do we know we are on Planet Zorg?'

'Now is not the time to make funny faces, Suzie!' Frank chastised me. 'And it is OBVIOUS. Replicators originate from Planet Zorg. They can be found all over the universe, but this is their home planet.'

'That is why there are so many of them! Now, you, turn back to your true form!' said Spaceman Jack, whacking the nearest replicator – a Five-Eyed Frank – on the head three times. The Five-Eyed Frank shimmered back into its gecko-like form. It waggled its tail at Spaceman Jack, who laughed.

'You try it, Suzie,' said Captain Jane encouragingly.

You know what is weirder than staring at a creature that looks exactly like you? Whacking one on the head.

'Are you sure it won't try and whack

me back?' I said, creeping up to the other Suzie. I didn't know if I would win in a fight against myself.

'Replicators are peaceful beings. Mischievous, but peaceful,' said Captain Jane.

I stared at the other Suzie. She stared back at me, and I swear she blinked at the same time I did. 'At least they can't mimic our voices,' I said. And then before I lost my nerve, I reached out and bonked the other Suzie on the head three times.

The other Suzie's head didn't feel like my head, with a hard human skull. Instead it felt like squishy rubber. She grinned at me, like she had been expecting me to do that and was in on the joke, and then shimmered into her gecko form. This one was purple with a green stripe down its back, and stood as tall as the others. It grinned at me again, this time with all of its teeth, and then turned to Captain Jane.

'No, you don't,' she said, pressing a button. A beam of light shone out of her spacesuit, straight into the replicator's eyes. 'Lighting their eyes confuses them, and they can't replicate what they see,' she explained to me.

The replicator squeaked in protest, but the light trick worked. It didn't replicate. Instead it slunk back into the forest, tail dragging behind it.

'Now, Frank,' said Captain Jane. 'How sure are you that we are on Planet Zorg?'

Frank began listing things on his fingers. 'Well, Planet Zorg is famous for three things: being home of the replicators, the colour-changing giant grass, and –'

'KNOWLEDGE WORMS!' I burst out.
I suddenly remembered Five-Eyed Frank
telling me about knowledge worms back
on TUBS. 'If we find the knowledge worms,
maybe they can tell us how we can fix TUBS!'

'Excellent idea,' said Captain Jane.

'Frank was the one who figured out
where we were,' I said, giving Frank a
wide smile. I felt like our experience so far
on Zorg had really bonded us. But then
my smile faltered. 'How will we find the
knowledge worms, though? They could be
ANYWHERE on the planet!'

'Three-Headed Tommy will be able to
sniff them out,' said Spaceman Jack. 'He's
got a great nose for this kind of thing.' He
laughed. 'Actually, he's got *three* great
noses! And three noses are better than
one!' He turned to the flying lizard. 'What

do you think, Tommy? Can you sniff out some knowledge worms?'

Tommy chirped and all three of his heads nodded. Then he landed on the ground and began to sniff around, burying one head in the dirt while the other two noses sniffed the air.

A few moments later he let out a loud, excited chirp and flew up into the air, all three of his mouths smiling as he did three jubilant flips.

'He's got the scent!' said Spaceman Jack. 'Follow him!'

We raced through the tall, wavy grass, careful to stay close together so we wouldn't get separated again.

A few replicators saw us. One turned itself into a replica of Tommy, but we knew which Tommy was real. The grass began to get shorter, and shorter, until it was only ankle-high, and then it wasn't there at all and we were in an enormous clearing. In the middle of the clearing was what looked like the entrance to an underground cave.

Tommy flew to the hole in the ground and let out three sharp chirps.

'Jumpin' Jupiter, I can't fit in there!' said Spaceman Jack, frowning at the hole.

'Me neither,' said Captain Jane.

'I might be able to,' I said, peering at the

hole, and trying to sound more brave than
I felt.

'Frank, I bet you could fit too,' said Captain Jane.

'Negative!' howled Frank. 'I don't want to go down there in the dark BY MYSELF!'

'You won't be by yourself,' said Spaceman Jack. 'You'll have Suzie and Tommy with you.'

'Didn't you say you always wanted to meet a knowledge worm? This is your chance!' I added.

Five-Eyed Frank let out a long sigh. 'I suppose you are right. But you have to go first, Suzie! Just in case Tommy is wrong and there is something else down in that cave.'

CHAPTER 8

DOWN INTO THE DARK

I was really nervous about going into the cave first, but it was important! We had to find the knowledge worms so we could figure out what was wrong with TUBS and get back into space. There was still a distant planet sending out a distress signal, after all.

Plus, if we never got back on to TUBS, how would I ever get home? We needed to fix TUBS for the greater good, but also so I had half a chance of returning to Earth.

Still, I hesitated. The cave entrance looked like a bottomless hole in the ground.

'You can do it, Suzie,' said Captain Jane, putting a reassuring hand on my shoulder. 'We believe in you. You are clever, kind and brave, all qualities that will make the knowledge worms want to help you. They know everything, remember? And so when they meet you, they'll know the kind of person you are.'

I swallowed down my nervousness. Captain Jane was right. I could do this.

I nodded at her, and then flung my hand up in the air in the Space Blasters, salute. 'For the universe!' I said. Captain Jane and Spaceman Jack did the same, and a

FUN FACT!

The largest cave in the world is the Son Doong Cave, located in Vietnam.

66

moment later Five-Eyed Frank joined in.

Then Captain Jane tied a rope around my waist to make sure I didn't get lost in the cave searching for knowledge worms. She looped the same rope around Frank's waist too.

'This way you two won't lose each other,' she said. 'Suzie will lead the way, and Frank will make sure nothing sneaks up on you.'

'WHAT?' squeaked Frank. 'Why is that my job?'

'That is always the job of the crew member who goes last,' said Spaceman Jack, patting Frank on the back. 'You just didn't know because you usually go in the middle. But you two make a great team. Don't worry. And Three-Headed Tommy is going down with you too. He'll help you sniff out those knowledge worms!'

'And Frank, don't forget to use your glowing fingertips,' said Captain Jane.

'What am I? A walking, talking torchlight?' grumbled Five-Eyed Frank, but his fingers sparked and glowed.

'And if you need help, press this button on your suit,' Captain Jane said to me. 'This will send out a distress signal.'

'And we'll come to your rescue,' said Spaceman Jack, striking a superhero pose.

'No offence, but if you can't fit through the cave entrance . . . how will you save us?' I said.

'We'll figure something out,' said Captain

Jane. 'We always do. But hopefully all will go smoothly and you'll be back up here in no time. And the knowledge worms will have told you how we can fix TUBS.'

'Great,' I said, forcing a smile. It suddenly felt like a LOT of pressure. What if we couldn't find the knowledge worms? What if we got stuck underground? What if there was some other scary creature waiting for us in the tunnels?

My smile must have faltered because Captain Jane crouched down next to me and gave my shoulder a reassuring squeeze. 'Don't worry, Suzie,' she said. 'You can do this. We believe in you, remember?'

'What about me?' squawked Five-Eyed Frank indignantly.

'We believe in you too,' said Spaceman Jack. 'Now hurry on down there! The

sooner you find those knowledge worms, the sooner we can get back to the stars!'

I stepped into the hole in the ground. I was expecting to fall a long way down, but it was more like walking down a very steep ramp. After a moment, the rope around my waist went taut. Where was Frank?

'Frank?' I called, looking back over my shoulder. 'Are you coming?'

Spaceman Jack and Captain Jane poked their heads into my field of vision. 'He's on his way!' said Spaceman Jack. And then Five-Eyed Frank was there behind me. A moment later, Tommy flew down too and settled on my shoulder.

I took one more look up at Captain Jane and Spaceman Jack, and then continued down the tunnel. 'Let's go, Frank!' I said. 'We've got a mission to do!'

'I hate being underground,' Frank grumbled back at me.

'We'll be OK,' I said confidently.

But the further we wound our way underground, the darker it grew, and there was no sign of knowledge worms anywhere. The edges of the tunnel were getting tighter too, and pretty soon my shoulders were scraping against the walls.

'Hey, Frank,' I said. 'Any chance you can make your fingertips glow a little brighter?'

Frank muttered under his breath, but a few moments later the tunnel lit up. 'I can see in the dark, you know,' he said. 'This is only for *your* benefit.'

The light reassured me. 'Well, I really appreciate it,' I said. 'Maybe when we are back on TUBS I can make it up to –'

Before I could finish my sentence, the ground beneath my feet gave way, and

I tumbled

down

into

the

dark.

'SUZIE!' Frank cried.

After a moment I stopped falling, suspended in mid-air.

I was hanging by the rope around my waist. It was tight – so tight it felt like it was cutting into my spacesuit – but I could breathe. I glanced up and even though I was terrified, couldn't help but grin at what I saw.

Five-Eyed Frank had both his arms and legs braced against the walls, supporting us both. The glowing tips of his fingers and surprisingly long toes were clinging to either side of the tunnel, and I could see he was trembling from holding my weight.

'Phew!' I said, trying to sound more relaxed than I was. 'That was close!'

'You are lucky I have sticky fingers and toes!' said Five-Eyed Frank.

Tommy chirped in agreement, and flew around my face, licking my cheek to comfort me as I dangled in the middle of the cavern.

Then he chirped again, louder this time, and all three of his heads swivelled in the same direction. And he dived down even deeper into the darkness.

'TOMMY! GET BACK HERE! WE CAN'T LOSE YOU!' cried Frank. 'SPACEMAN JACK WOULD NEVER FORGIVE ME!'

'We aren't going to lose Tommy!' I said.

'BUT WE CAN'T GO ANY DEEPER IN THIS CAVE! WHAT IF HE NEVER COMES BACK?'

'Of course he's coming back,' I said, still dangling as I tried to peer down into the depths to see where the three-headed lizard had gone. 'He's just investigating!' Then it hit me. 'He must have found the knowledge worms!'

'He has indeed,' said a new voice from below me.

CHAPTER 9

KNOWLEDGE WORMS

I yelped and looked down.

Far below me something was moving.

Lots of somethings.

As I stared down, trying to see better, Three-Headed Tommy suddenly flew up from the darkness, chirping with excitement and kicking his legs around my face.

'WHAT IS GOING ON DOWN THERE?' cried Five-Eyed Frank.

'I don't know! I'm trying to see!' I yelled back.

'We will tell you what is going on,' said the voice again. The voice was low and deep. It rumbled all around me and I felt it echo in my bones. 'We are the knowledge worms.'

I gasped in surprise. I hadn't expected them to speak.

'And we know you have come to us with a problem you need help solving.' As my eyes grew more used to the darkness, I saw shapes moving below me. The knowledge worms were silver, and glowing faintly in the dark cave. I realised they were making a kind of knowledge worm ladder, crawling on to each other so I would be able to speak face to face with the ones on top.

The worm at the very top of the stack had nearly reached me. It wriggled to its full height. It was far bigger than a normal worm. When it was fully stretched out, it looked like it was taller than me, but not as tall as Captain Jane or Spaceman Jack.

The rest of the worms writhed around beneath it, keeping the top worm elevated.

The worm was a pale silver like the rest of them, and when it opened its eyes, silver light shone out, as if it had a torch inside its head.

The eyes seemed to scan me.

'You are a human,' it said. 'How peculiar. We have never met a human before.'

The worms below murmured in agreement.

The top worm's glowing eyes scanned Five-Eyed Frank next. 'And you are a five-eyed, colour-changing species with star-tipped fingers from the most distant galaxy in the universe. You are called . . .' The

knowledge worm paused, clearly thinking.

'Excuse me!' said Five-Eyed Frank a bit frantically. 'What kind of species I am is not any of your business!'

I stared up at Frank. 'You can change colours? And you have star-tip fingers? And you are from the most distant galaxy?' I had SO many questions for him!

Five-Eyed Frank simply glared back at me.

The knowledge worm let out a sound that I think was a laugh. 'We are knowledge worms. We know all. All is our business. Which is a colloquial phrase for being interested or invested in another creature.' The worm's head swivelled back to me. 'Now, tell us why you are here.'

Still dangling by my waist, I quickly told the knowledge worms everything that had happened to TUBS.

The knowledge worm closed its eyes for a long moment. It began to vibrate with energy, and small glowing beads began to appear on its skin.

'Smart pellets!' yelped Five-Eyed Frank. 'Those are smart pellets! Knowledge worms excrete them when they are thinking! They are extremely rare! Grab one!'

I hesitated because it didn't seem very polite just to take something off another creature, especially when that creature was helping you.

'Is . . . is that OK?' I asked the knowledge worm.

It opened its eyes, the strange light shining out at me. 'Because you asked, you may,' it answered. 'But take no more than three. They are heavier than they look. And do not eat more than one at once.

Knowledge is powerful. Even if the effects only last for ninety seconds.'

I gingerly plucked off three of the smart pellets, which were still damp from the knowledge worm's skin. They were a little squishy, but hardened quickly into round, hard, shimmery pellets. I slipped them inside a pocket of my spacesuit.

'And as for your problem, I know the answer. Your ship has an infestation of moon bugs,' said the knowledge worm. 'It is the only thing that would cause a spaceship to act like that.'

I'd never heard of moon bugs, and I had about a million more questions that I wanted to ask the knowledge worms. But only one question was important.

'Will you come and help us get rid of the infestation?' The knowledge worms would know exactly how to do it, since they knew everything!

To my dismay, the knowledge worm shook its head. 'We do not leave our underground home.'

'But you could do ANYTHING with your knowledge!' I burst out. 'Solve all the problems in the universe!'

'We think. That is what we do. We think, and we answer those who seek us out. We spend all of our energy thinking. And when we are not thinking, we are resting.' The light behind the knowledge worm's eyes began to dim. 'And now we must rest. And you must leave.'

'But I have more questions!' I said. 'We don't know how to get rid of the moon bugs! And I don't know how to get home!'

My voice echoed around the cavern.

'We have exerted ourselves to think on your spaceship problem. Now we must sleep,' the knowledge worm said. 'And you must leave, otherwise you will be stuck down here until the cave opens again. You see, the grass on Zorg is not the only thing that shifts.'

'What do you mean?' I asked a little nervously.

As the knowledge worm answered, the rocky cavern walls began to tremble. 'The tunnel you came through is now closing. The ground on Zorg is unstable. We stay safe down here because we know which tunnels to seek. But the tunnel we are travelling to next is not suitable for you. It is deep, deep beneath Zorg.'

The knowledge worm closed its eyes. Another smart pellet appeared on its body, and I knew it was thinking hard about something. Then its eyes snapped open and they were at full brightness again.

'Earthling, you have exactly three minutes and forty-two seconds to get back to the surface.' The knowledge worm blinked. 'Make that three minutes and forty seconds. Hurry.'

Then it closed its eyes and dropped

back down on to the mountain of writhing knowledge worms beneath it. Then the worms all began to wriggle down to the depths of the cavern, their silver bodies glowing faintly in the dark.

The whole cavern shuddered again, and a piece of falling rock hit me on the shoulder.

'COME ON, SUZIE!' shouted Five-Eyed Frank from above me. 'YOU HEARD THE KNOWLEDGE WORM! WE HAVE TO GET OUT OF HERE!'

I didn't know what to do! I was dangling in mid-air with less than three minutes and forty seconds to get out of a collapsing cavern.

Frank was using all his energy to keep me from falling even deeper in. I didn't know if he was strong enough to haul me back up. Three-Headed Tommy was chirping in alarm and flying wildly around my face.

'Three minutes and twenty seconds,' said a voice from deep in the cavern.

'TELL ME HOW TO GET OUT!' I yelled back.

'The star-tip alien can use his star-tip fingers and toes to blast you out of here. The propulsion will provide enough energy to lift you both through the tunnel.'

'Frank?' I yelled.

'I've never done that before!' Frank yelled back. 'I didn't even know I could!' His voice grew quiet. 'Nobody ever taught me how to use my star-tip fingers and toes. I've had to figure it out by myself.'

FUN FACT!

Propulsion is the action of driving or pushing forwards – propulsion is the force that sends a rocket into space!

'Well, you can do this. It is something every star-tip alien can do.' The voice of the knowledge worm sounded further away now, almost echoing in the distance. 'It is simple. The human is already attached to you by the rope. Focus on your star-tip fingers and toes and use them to propel your way out.' There was a pause. 'You have less than three minutes. This is the only way you can get out of the tunnel in time.'

'COME ON, FRANK!' I shouted. 'You can do it! I believe in you!'

Frank scrunched up his face in concentration. 'This is why I don't like to leave the ship!' he shouted. 'THINGS ALWAYS GET WEIRD!'

'Hold on tight, human,' said the knowledge worm from somewhere far beneath me.

And then Five-Eyed Frank's fingers and toes lit up so bright I had to close my eyes, and with a whoosh, he shot upwards through the tunnel, with me flying behind him like a comet tail.

CHAPTER 10

MEET THE
MOON BUGS

We burst up out of the tunnel and landed in a heap on the wavy, purple grass.

Three-Headed Tommy flew up right after us. Moments later, the ground lurched, and the tunnel we had just emerged from shuddered shut, like it had never been there at all.

'Jumpin' Jupiter! That was close!' said Spaceman Jack, rushing over to us. 'You three were nearly flattened like pancakes!'

'Are you all right?' said Captain Jane,

90

kneeling down next to me.

I rolled over on my back, trying to catch my breath. 'I think so,' I said.

'I'll check your vitals,' said Captain Jane.

'Frank? Are your fingers . . . smoking?' said Spaceman Jack slowly.

Five-Eyed Frank waved his fingers in the air, and I saw that they were indeed gently smoking. 'Apparently,' he said. 'And no wonder! Did YOU know my fingers could be used as mini rockets?'

Spaceman Jack shook his head. 'No, sir. I knew they could light up, and could work as lasers, same as you, but little rockets? WOW! You sure are full of surprises.'

'The knowledge

FUN FACT!

Vitals, or vital signs, are signs of life! They measure a body's most basic functions. They include blood pressure, heart rate, temperature and breathing rate.

worm said Five-Eyed Frank had "star-tip" fingers,' I explained. 'They knew he could blast us out of there before the tunnel closed!'

'So you found the knowledge worms? Well done,' said Captain Jane. 'Did they tell you anything useful?'

'Of course we found them,' said Five-Eyed Frank in a grumpy voice. 'That was the whole reason we went down there.'

'Well, you came blasting out of there so fast, we weren't sure if you'd had to give up on the mission,' said Spaceman Jack.

'I WOULD NEVER GIVE UP ON A MISSION!' exclaimed Five-Eyed Frank. He frowned. 'Just because I don't like leaving the spaceship doesn't mean I'm the kind of alien who gives up!'

'You were very brave, Frank,' I said. 'You

saved us both.' I pulled myself up into a sitting position and held my hand to his still slightly smoking one. 'Palm five!'

Five-Eyed Frank gave me a tentative grin, and then we palm-fived. 'I was awesome, wasn't I?' he said.

'Extremely awesome,' I agreed, grinning widely back at him. Then I turned to Spaceman Jack and Captain Jane. 'We found the knowledge worms thanks to Three-Headed Tommy! He led us to their cavern.'

'And did they know what was wrong with TUBS?' asked Captain Jane.

A bit breathlessly, I told Captain Jane and Spaceman Jack everything that had happened, and what was apparently wrong with TUBS.

'What is a moon bug anyway?' I said after I'd finished. 'The knowledge worms

didn't explain in detail.' I could have eaten
one of the smart pellets in my pocket
to figure out what moon bugs were,
but I figured I should save them for an
emergency.

'Moon bugs are the garbage collectors of
the universe,' Spaceman Jack explained.
He suddenly looked extremely nervous. His
face shone with sweat and his eyes kept
darting around.

'But we aren't on a moon,' I said.

'They usually live on moons but they
float through space and eat up any space
debris they can find,' said Captain Jane.
'They help keep the entire universe tidy.'

'Ohhh!' I said. 'Like cleaner fish!'

'What is a cleaner fish?' said Five-Eyed
Frank, wrinkling his nose.

'I learned about them watching a nature

94

show,' I said, proud that I was able to offer some useful information. 'They are little fish that eat parasites off big fish. And the big fish know that the little fish are helping them, so they don't try and eat them. They are really important to the ocean's ecosystem and help keep the oceans on

Earth clean.'

'Well, moon bugs don't usually clean other aliens – instead they eat space debris and space rubbish. They are very useful,' said Captain Jane. 'It is strange for them to be on our spaceship, though I've never heard of a moon-bug infestation. It is usually considered good luck if you see one.'

'It probably isn't a moon-bug infestation,' said Spaceman Jack quickly. 'The knowledge worms must have been wrong.'

'Knowledge worms are never wrong,' said Five-Eyed Frank. 'They know everything, remember?'

'Well, maybe they made a mistake this time. I, for one, do not think this is why TUBS crash-landed. There has to be another reason.' Spaceman Jack was really sweating now.

I suddenly remembered the strange giggling I'd heard in the ship.

'There is definitely something in the walls of the ship,' I said, and then told the rest of the crew what I had heard.

'Only one way to find out,' said Captain Jane, and then she went and knocked hard on the side of TUBS. 'This is Captain Jane, and this is a formal request to speak to a moon bug. I repeat, this is Captain Jane, and this is a formal request from the captain of this ship.'

All of TUBS shuddered.

'TUBS will try to listen to the command,' Five-Eyed Frank explained to me. 'Even if it has shut down, a spaceship does everything it can to listen to its captain.'

TUBS shuddered again, like it was having

some sort of battle inside itself. Then a small side panel sprang open, and a little creature popped out and rolled on to the ground.

'Well, that is definitely a moon bug,' said Five-Eyed Frank.

'It is so cute!' I said.

The moon bug looked like a cross between a ladybird, a bumble bee and a stag beetle. It was about the size of a tennis ball, had a round head on top of a round body, and two curved antennae that almost looked like horns sprouting from the top of its head. It had two big eyes that took up most of its face, and lots of little

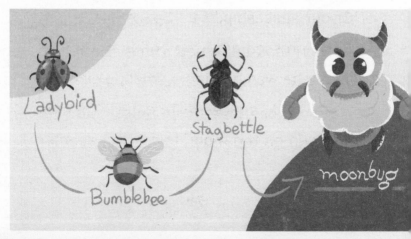

Ladybird

Bumblebee

Stagbettle

moonbug

legs poking out from underneath its body.
This one was green with bright yellow polka
dots. Two jagged front teeth, sort of like
walrus tusks, poked out of its mouth.

I reached over to it.

'WATCH OUT!' cried Spaceman Jack,
just as the moon bug unhinged its jaws.
Suddenly it was ALL mouth and teeth.

It bounced towards me and I scrambled
back. 'How is its mouth so big?'

'Moon bugs can change size,' said
Captain Jane. 'It means they can shrink
down small enough to get into all the nooks
and crannies of a space rock.'

'Or our spaceship,' said Spaceman
Jack. He pressed a button on his suit and
suddenly he was holding a small, glowing
net. 'Get back, space-waste eater!' The net
came down on the moon bug and it seemed

to get even angrier.

'But they don't get any bigger than this,' said Captain Jane.

'And thank goodness for that,' said Spaceman Jack. 'Can you imagine a giant moon bug coming at you?'

'I WOULD SWALLOW YOU WHOLE!' screeched the moon bug.

I jumped back even further. 'They talk?'

'Yes! We do talk! And I have a message from the queen! She says ALL of the universe will know that YOU, Spaceman Jack from Earth, are the reason we have decided to eat EVERYTHING!'

'Wait, what?' I said, staring at Spaceman Jack. 'What is the moon bug talking about?'

The moon bug suddenly shrank right before my eyes, until it was no bigger than an eraser on the top of a pencil. But its voice still echoed.

'Spaceman Jack thinks he is a hero! But soon all will despise him as WE despise him! Spaceman Jack will pay for what he did to Queen Moon Bug!'

The moon bug slipped out of the net. Four wings opened on its back and it flew up and into Spaceman Jack's face.

Spaceman Jack swatted at the moon

bug, but it was too fast for him.

'YOU WILL KNOW OUR WRATH!'
it shrieked, and then it turned and
disappeared back inside TUBS.

Spaceman Jack chased it and banged on
the door of TUBS. 'Let me into my ship!' he
cried. 'I have to get that moon bug!'

But TUBS didn't respond.

'It belongs to the moon bugs now,' said
Frank grimly. 'I bet opening up to let that
moon bug out was the last thing TUBS was
able to do for us.'

'Jack,' said Captain Jane very slowly.
'Why does Queen Moon Bug hate you?'

Spaceman Jack ran a hand through his
hair. His shoulders slumped. 'It's kind of a
long story,' he said.

'Well, as we can't go anywhere because
our ship is broken due to a moon-bug

infestation that sounds like *your* fault, I think we have plenty of time for you to tell it,' said Captain Jane.

Spaceman Jack turned towards us with a pout. 'Do I have to?'

'That's an order, spaceman,' said Captain Jane. 'We need to know what we are dealing with.'

'Here,' I said, opening my backpack to take out some dried fruit that I'd stashed earlier. 'Why don't we have some snacks while you tell us? Snacks make everything better.'

'For once, I agree with Suzie,' said Five-Eyed Frank. 'And I can't even eat any of that.'

'Don't worry, Frank,' I said, digging deeper into my backpack. 'I brought some bolts just for you!'

Five-Eyed Frank ate nails and bolts and sometimes space worms. So when I had packed the snacks for us, I made sure to grab something for him too.

His eyes grew wide. 'That is very nice,' he said.

'I'll have some dried mango,' said Spaceman Jack, reaching out his hand. He chewed for a long moment.

'Less snacking, more explaining,' said Captain Jane sternly.

Spaceman Jack sighed again and sat down beside TUBS.

'It all started when we landed on Planet Toby for the Intergalactic Card Tournament . . .'

CHAPTER 11

THE INTERGALACTIC CARD TOURNAMENT

'I had been preparing for the Intergalactic Card Tournament every chance I got,' said Spaceman Jack. He glanced over at Frank. 'You remember, right, Frank? We played all the time. We did shoo-bop –'

'What is shoo-bop?' I felt a little bad for interrupting the story right at the start, but I couldn't help myself. I had to know what shoo-bop was!

Spaceman Jack brightened. 'Oh, it is the best! We'll have to play some time. You know what, I might even have some cards somewhere in my spacesuit . . .' He began to pat around on his suit.

'No shoo-bop!' ordered Captain Jane. 'Keep telling the story.'

'I was just answering the question,' said Spaceman Jack defensively. 'These are important details!' He turned back to me. 'Shoo-bop is a game of skill and luck. You use space cards, and each one does a little trick depending on where it is from in the universe. So, a card from a really hot planet might burst into flames. Or a card from a planet with low gravity would float. You have to line the cards up in a way to make them work together. And if you are really good at it, and of course I am, you don't lose any cards.'

'That sounds even harder than space

chess,' I said.

Spaceman Jack chuckled. 'It does take a while to get the hang of it. And collecting your deck is a mission in itself! I remember when I picked up my first water card –'

'Back to the story about the moon bugs, Spaceman Jack,' said Captain Jane.

'Right,' said Spaceman Jack. 'So there I was, ready for the first round of shoo-bop. I had all my cards lined up, and I look up to see who I'm playing, and it's the queen of the moon bugs! I didn't even know moon bugs could play cards! I was so surprised that I told her so.'

'I'm guessing she didn't like that,' I said, cringing a little bit just thinking about it.

'No, she did not,' agreed Spaceman Jack.

'And that is why she now wants to devour the entire universe and say you are to blame? Because you said moon bugs couldn't play cards?' asked Captain Jane sceptically.

Spaceman Jack gave us a sheepish grin.

'No. That is just to show you that we got off to a terrible start. So I say this, and the queen of the moon bugs just glares at me, doesn't say a word, and gets out her deck. And it is the most impressive shoo-bop deck I've ever seen! It has cards from planets I've never even heard of. But I'm not worried, because I know my deck is strong. I've been practising. Nobody beats me at shoo-bop, not even the queen of the moon bugs. Not a chance.'

'Where was I when all this was

happening?' said Captain Jane, her frown deepening.

'You and Frank were watching the rocket race,' said Spaceman Jack. 'Anyway, I decide that I'm going to win Queen Moon Bug's shoo-bop cards. We start the traditional way, one card versus one card, and – exploding cosmos, she takes half my deck! Her cards are doing things I've never even seen. No matter what card I put up, she beats me! I'm running out of cards, and quick. Remember, I have built up my deck over time, and it pains me to be losing all these cards. So then I do something that I'm not too proud of.' Spaceman Jack blushed so hard even the tips of his ears turned red. 'I say she's cheating.'

Five-Eyed Frank, Captain Jane and I all gasp.

'I say that she's got her moon-bug minions spying on my cards, guessing my next move, and that they are too small for me to see,' Spaceman Jack goes on. 'And Queen Moon Bug, well, she doesn't like that. Not that I blame her. But then the game comes to a halt, and the head judge of the Intergalactic Card Tournament is called over. And he asks for proof. And he says one of us is going to get kicked out of the tournament for life. And things have escalated really quickly. I'm not expecting any of this to happen, I just want to get some of my hard-won cards back.'

'Sounds like hard-lost,' said Frank.

'But then I couldn't back down, could I?' said Spaceman Jack, looking more and more embarassed. 'I have a card that has a little bite out of it. It isn't from a moon bug – this card got bitten by a biting card from Planet Teeth – but the head judge doesn't know that. And I say . . . I say it is a moon-bug bite.'

'SPACEMAN JACK! Lying is against the Space Blasters, code!' Captain Jane bursts out.

'I know, I know,' mutters Spaceman Jack. 'But I wasn't on TUBS. I wasn't thinking. And then – well, Queen Moon Bug got so angry she went ALL teeth, you know how moon bugs do, and it kind of accidentally proved my point, and they took her shoo-bop cards AND they banned her and all the moon bugs from ever taking part in the Intergalactic Card Tournament again . . .'

'And did you speak up and say it was big misunderstanding?' I said hopefully. 'Come to the rescue?'

Spaceman Jack looked down at his space boots. 'No. I, erm, said she was a space-trash eater and I took her deck. Then she looked me right in the eye and said, "You'll regret this, spaceman," and at the time I thought I wouldn't because the universe is a big place and I thought she'd never find me. But she has.'

'Didn't you feel bad?' I asked.
I remembered one time when I was playing Monopoly with my brother and sister and they accused *me* of cheating, just because they couldn't believe that they were being beaten by someone younger than them, and I was so upset I cried for two hours and then my mum took away the game and

never let us play again. Worst of all, my brother and sister blamed me, even though I hadn't done anything at all. Just thinking about it made a lump rise in my throat. We hadn't played Monopoly since that day. 'You should have admitted you were lying!'

'Well,' Spaceman Jack blustered, 'then I would have been banned from playing in the Intergalactic Card Tournament, and I love it so much!"

'So this is absolutely, one hundred per cent, your fault,' said Captain Jane, rubbing at a worry line between her eyes.

Spaceman Jack blinked. 'I mean, I'll take some of the blame. But surely not all of it? Things just got out of hand, you know how that can happen . . .'

'I'm pretty sure it is all your fault,' I said. I couldn't believe Spaceman Jack had

accused

Queen Moon Bug

of cheating!

'You need to apologise. Right now.'
Captain Jane strode up to the side of TUBS
and banged on it. 'Hello! Queen Moon Bug?
This is Captain Jane of the Space Blasters.
My crew member Spaceman Jack has
something to say to you.'

TUBS shuddered and a small moon
bug flew out. This one was hot pink with
neon-blue spots. 'WE WILL DEVOUR THE
UNIVERSE AND ALL WILL KNOW IT IS
BECAUSE SPACEMAN JACK IS A LIAR.'

Another small moon bug flew out.
'SHAME ON YOU! SHAME ON YOU!'

More and more poured out of the cracks

in TUBS until it was an entire swarm all around us, and we didn't even swat at them because we knew that they were right. Their voices grew louder until it was all I could hear.

'ALL WILL BE DEVOURED!'

Spaceman Jack had made a very dangerous, very tiny enemy, and the entire universe was going to suffer for it.

Something had to be done. Someone had to save the day.

And I had just the idea for how to do it.

CHAPTER 12

SMART PELLETS

'RUN AWAY!' cried Spaceman Jack, still swatting with his net. 'There are too many of them!'

We all ran away from TUBS and into the tall grass.

'I don't believe we have just been chased away from our spaceship by moon bugs!' said Five-Eyed Frank with a groan. 'How will we ever get our ship back?'

'Those moon bugs are really mad at you, Spaceman Jack,' said Captain Jane, looking extremely unhappy. 'I've told you that your actions have consequences.'

'I know! I know!' wailed Spaceman Jack, burying his face in his hands. 'This is all my fault! What are we going to do?'

'We can't even go back to the knowledge worms to ask how one removes a moon-bug infestation until the ground shifts again on Planet Zorg,' said Frank. 'And who knows how long that will take?' He looked longingly in the direction of TUBS. 'I miss my bed! And the canteen! And being up in the stars!'

'We'll figure something out,' said Captain Jane with a sigh.

'I have an idea,' I said. 'I think I know how I can fix this!'

Everyone turned and stared at me.

'I'll have to eat a smart pellet though,' I admitted.

'Oh, Suzie! That isn't how smart pellets work. You won't be able to magically solve every problem in the universe by eating one,' said Five-Eyed Frank, rolling his eyes.

'I know how to solve the moon-bug problem,' I insisted. 'What I don't know is how to turn myself into a moon bug.'

And then I told them my plan.

Ten minutes later, Captain Jane still wasn't sure it was a good idea.

'Suzie, what if you stay stuck as a moon bug?' she said. 'One of us should do it. Me, or Spaceman Jack . . .'

'Absolutely not,' said Spaceman Jack quickly. 'This famous smile is not meant to be on a moon bug!' He flashed us all a smile, as if to prove his point.

'Besides, I'm pretty sure Queen Moon Bug would lock him up at first sight,' I said. 'It has to be me! The moon bugs have never met me. They have no reason to hate me. They won't like either of you because they know you are friends with Spaceman Jack, but I'm new to them!'

Captain Jane sighed and pushed a curl behind her ear. 'It is too dangerous, Suzie.'

I shook my head. 'It isn't! The smart pellets will tell me how to turn into a moon bug, and how to do it safely. I'm sure of it!'

'I think she can do it,' said Five-Eyed Frank.

I gave him a suspicious glance.

'Is that because you want me to be stuck as a moon bug?'

Five-Eyed Frank laughed. 'No! Of course not. It is because you are clever. That is a good idea. And if you DO get stuck as a moon bug – well, I'll go underground again, even though I absolutely do not want to, and I'll find a knowledge worm to figure out how to change you back into a human.'

I felt my eyes fill with unexpected tears. It was the nicest thing Five-Eyed Frank had ever said to me.

'You are part of the crew, remember?' he said. 'And we look out for each other!'

'Frank is right,' said Spaceman Jack. 'Suzie can do this.'

'You are just happy somebody else is going to clean up your mess,' said Captain Jane. Then she sighed deeply. 'Do you really think you can convince Queen Moon Bug, Suzie?'

'If I can turn myself into a moon bug, I think I can,' I said confidently. 'I'll explain everything to the queen. I'm good at explaining things, remember?'

'She really is,' said Spaceman Jack. 'And I'm not just saying that because I want her to clean up my mess! I mean . . . I do want her to fix the situation with the moon bugs, but also, Suzie really is good at fixing things.'

'It's true,' said Frank.

Even Tommy chirped in agreement.

'OK, I'll let you do this,' said Captain Jane. 'But don't make me regret it.'

'You can count on me, Captain!' I said, saluting.

We made our way deeper into the tall grass, making sure to stay together so we wouldn't be separated like when we'd first arrived on Planet Zorg.

'OK,' I said, taking out one of the smart

pellets. 'Here goes! In three minutes I'll know exactly how I can turn into a moon bug.'

I put the smart pellet in my mouth and tried to forget that it had basically been sweated out by the knowledge worm.

As soon as I swallowed it, my brain felt like it had grown A MILLION TIMES.

I knew *EVERYTHING.*

Focus, focus, focus. I told myself. *FOCUS.*

But there were so many facts I wanted to know! My brain was whirring so fast, and as soon as I had a question, it was answered!

How hot is the Earth's sun? 15 million Celsius.

How old is the oldest tree on Planet Earth?
In California, there is a tree that is 4,853 years old!

How are black holes in space formed?
When a very big star dies, it implodes and collapses on itself, resulting in a black hole.

What causes a rainbow? Rainbows are formed when light shines through water. The light is bent and reflected resulting in the colours of a rainbow!

What is the difference between a frog and a toad?
A frog has moist, smooth skin and long legs. A toad has dry, rough skin and shorter legs.

How big is a blue whale? Between 24 to 33 metres! That is as long as three buses lined up!

How many bones does a shark have?
ZERO! A shark does not have a single bone in its body and is made entirely of cartilage — the same things human ears and noses are made out of.

I wanted to keep thinking up questions as fast as I could, but I knew I was running out of time. The smart pellet only worked for ninety seconds.

I thought my question as hard as I could: *How can I turn into a moon bug?*

Instead of words, images filled my head.

I saw a replicator open its mouth and spit out a big glob of slime. Yuck! And then I saw an image of myself spreading the replicator slime all over me.

Oh no! I needed to cover myself in replicator slime! They had the same guanine crystals in their cells that chameleons had, and it was in their slime. If I coated myself in it, I would have the same ability to replicate!

Whoa. Before this moment I hadn't even known what a guanine crystal was. And

now I did! Suddenly
my brain was telling
me all about guanine
crystals and how
replicators changed
colour. Replicators, and

FUN FACT!

Guanine is one of the
four building blocks of
DNA: and DNA is what
all life forms, on Earth
at least, are made of!

chameleons, could rearrange

the cells on the top layer of their skin,

which meant they could then change colour

– or, in the case of the replicator, even their

whole shape! Guanine is used in nature for

camouflage! Just like I was going to use it!

I needed replicator slime, and also DNA

from a moon bug, and then I could turn

myself INTO a moon bug!

Replicator slime was more potent than

anything on Earth for replicating, so it was

lucky we were here on Planet Zorg. My

brain was in overdrive. I wanted to keep

thinking, keep figuring things out, but a voice kept interrupting my thoughts.

A voice that was getting louder and louder.

'YOU ONLY HAVE TEN MORE SECONDS!'

It was Frank! I focused my brain on my question until I was certain I knew the answer. It was going to be messy, but I could do it!

CHAPTER 13

MOON BUG ME

First, we had to catch a replicator.

'That won't be hard,' said Spaceman Jack with confidence. 'Replicators are curious creatures. They will want to find us again. All we need to do is wait for them.'

Captain Jane agreed. 'I don't want us splitting up again,' she said. 'And I want to be with Suzie when she turns herself into a moon bug.'

So we sat in a circle, and waited.

And waited.

Finally, a replicator snuck through the tall purple grass. It wasn't in its replicator form. Instead, it looked like Captain Jane.

'Suzie,' said Captain Jane quietly. 'Did you learn how they mimic appearance? Even from a distance?'

It was very strange to be talking to Captain Jane, while another creature that looked just like her strolled towards us.

'Replicators don't need to be touching a creature to take on their appearance,' I said, remembering what I'd learned from the smart pellet. 'They can scan them with their eyes, and then take on their appearance. Which is why shining light in their eyes can stop them from replicating. But I need to use their slime and some moon-bug DNA to be able to turn myself into a moon bug.'

The replicator walked up to us and

smirked, exactly the way Captain Jane would. Spaceman Jack calmly stood and bonked it on the head three times, and the replicator transformed into its original, gecko-like appearance. '*Blorp, blorp*,' it said as it assessed us.

'Listen, lizard pal, we need a favour,' said Spaceman Jack, casually nudging the replicator with his elbow, like they were old buddies hanging out. 'You can understand me, can't you?'

The replicator stared at Spaceman Jack with its huge eyes. '*Blorp*.'

'I don't know if they have the same level of communication skills as humans or other speaking species,' observed Five-Eyed Frank.

'All right, you big lizard lump,' said Spaceman Jack. 'Can you do this?'

He spat on the ground in front of them.

The replicator took a step back in alarm,
and then bared its teeth at Spaceman Jack.

'Spaceman Jack,' said Captain Jane
warningly. 'We do not want to start a battle
with another space species. Please do not
offend the replicators.'

I approached the replicator, lowered my
head respectfully, and gave it a little curtsey.
There was a faint rustling sound, and I knew
it had replicated to look like me.

I glanced up into my own eyes.

'Like this,' I said, and spat on the ground next to where Spaceman Jack had done it.

'Yuck,' said Five-Eyed Frank.

But the replicator was intrigued. It stared at me a moment longer, and then spat too.

'Yes, yes!' I said, clapping my hands. 'Like that!'

The replicator spit was thick and a faint blue. We took turns spitting, until I thought there was enough for me to coat all over myself.

The replicator seemed to think it was a game, and began to laugh. The sound was a bit like a cross between a caw and a hiss, and it was unnerving hearing a strange laugh coming out of a creature that looked like me.

'All right, buddy,' said Spaceman Jack. 'Time for you to shift back.'

To my surprise, the replicator turned back to its true form without needing to be bonked on the head. It gave me a wink, and then spat another huge glob of spit on to the floor, before it slunk away into the tall grass.

'Maybe it understood more than it let on,' I said.

'Most creatures do,' said Captain Jane.

I eyed the puddle of replicator spit and slime in front of me. 'Well, time to coat myself in that.'

Captain Jane and Spaceman Jack helped

me cover myself in the replicator slime.
Five-Eyed Frank watched from a distance,
wrinkling his nose in distaste. 'Ew. I would
not do that.'

'Well, lucky for you, you don't have to,'
I said, wrinkling my own nose as I got a
whiff of the slime. It smelled like wet shoes.
'Spaceman Jack, do you have that net that
you tried to catch the moon bugs with?'

Spaceman Jack nodded. 'Why?'

'Because that will have moon-bug DNA.
And with that, I'll be able to turn myself
into a moon bug!'

'Brilliant, Suzie!' said Captain Jane.

I knew I wouldn't be able to see the DNA
– it is too small to be seen – but I did see
a small scale from a moon bug's wing, like
a tiny piece of glitter. And the moon bug's
DNA would be on that.

I very carefully pressed my replicator-goop-covered finger to the small, shimmering scale – and gasped aloud as the goop absorbed the shining scale in an instant.

Be a moon bug, be a moon bug, be a moon bug, I thought to myself over and over.

And suddenly the replicator slime took on a life of its own.

It began to shake like jelly all around me, and then that tiny, shining scale began to replicate inside it. I let out a sharp cry as the goop covered my face entirely, and all I could see was sparkling replicator slime. And I had a moment of HUGE regret. What was I doing? What if this didn't work? What if I was suffocated by sparkling replicator goop infused with moon-bug DNA?

Captain Jane's voice came from very far away.

'Focus, Suzie! Think moon bug!'

Moon bug, moon bug, moon bug, I thought
over and over again as my whole body began
to tingle – and then there was a flash of bright
light, and then everything went still.

The replicator goop sloshed off me as
I took a step forward.

Whoa! I had six feet!

And I could see everything SUPER
well. Everything around me was crystal
clear. And my jaws! I opened my mouth
experimentally. And kept opening it. Wow.
I could fit a *lot* of dumplings into my moon-
bug mouth. And my jaws itched to bite into
something.

'IT WORKED!' shrieked a familiar voice.
A very LOUD familiar voice. Five-Eyed Frank
was right next to me and he was HUGE! 'You
are a moon bug! I can't believe it!'

'WATCH YOUR STEP!' I yelled back
at him. My own voice was much higher
pitched than usual.

Then Captain Jane was there, crouching
down beside me, and picking me up in her

hands. I let out a sigh of relief, knowing
I was safe with her.

But the feeling of safety only lasted a
moment. I knew I had to go into TUBS, find
the moon bugs and complete my mission.

'Suzie? Do you feel all right?' asked
Captain Jane.

'I . . . I think so!' I said. 'What do I look
like?'

Captain Jane assessed me. 'Like yourself,
but as a moon bug. You have the same
colour pattern as one of the moon bugs we
saw earlier, which makes sense since you
used its DNA to replicate.'

Five-Eyed Frank popped his head into
my field of vision. 'But your face is still
your face! Except your eyes are bigger.
And so is your mouth. I mean ALL of you
is smaller, but your eyes and mouth are

bigger proportionally than they were. Like a
moon-bug face.'

'That was the goal,' I said. 'To have a
moon-bug face.'

'It is still a Suzie face,' said Captain Jane
reassuringly.

'You are braver than I am,' said Spaceman Jack. 'My face wouldn't work on a moon bug.' Then he looked a bit sheepish. 'You still like me, right? Turning into a moon bug didn't make you automatically hate me?'

'Hmmm . . .' I said, narrowing my eyes at him. Then I laughed. 'Of course not! I'm still ME. Just in moon-bug form!'

'Now the only question is, how to get you into TUBS,' said Captain Jane.

'Oh, that part is easy,' said Spaceman Jack. 'TUBS is now apparently programmed to obey the moon bugs, and – well, we've got our very own moon bug.'

'For the universe!' I said, doing the rocket point with one of my small arms. Then I felt a prickling on my back.

'I HAVE WINGS!' I somehow knew how to open up my moon-bug wings, and I fluttered up towards TUBS. 'Hello! There's another moon bug out here! Please let me in!'

TUBS creaked open just enough for a moon bug to fly in.

This was it.

My only chance to find the moon bugs and convince them to forgive Spaceman Jack, leave TUBS alone, and get back to their job of eating space garbage.

It was up to me to save the crew. I wouldn't let them down. And before I could convince myself otherwise, I flew straight into TUBS.

CHAPTER 14

THE SECRET
SMALL CITY

Everything was so *bright.* I looked down to shield my eyes and realised that the floor was covered in thick wires. So many wires, I could barely even see the floor. I blinked a few times, adjusting my vision. When I looked up, I couldn't believe my eyes.

Instead of being inside the cabin of the ship, I was inside the *walls* of the ship. And it was like I had flown into some sort of futuristic super city. Moon bugs were

zipping everywhere. Some were flying
around, carrying nuts and bolts and bits
of shiny foil. Others were munching the
walls, their sharp teeth bared, making little
cubbies. I saw one of the moon bugs carry
a large piece of shiny foil into one of the
freshly made cubbies in the wall. It balled
the foil up and placed it on to the cubby

floor. Then it hopped up on top of the foil and snuggled down, wiggling its bum to sink into it. It smiled and closed its eyes, belching gently before falling asleep.

I gasped. The moon bugs were making nests in the walls! There were hundreds and hundreds of nests *everywhere.*

A purple moon bug with pink spots

zipped by me so fast that I almost tumbled over.

It stopped and turned round. 'Oh dear! Sorry, fellow moon bug! So, so sorry! I didn't see you there.'

The moon bug met my eyes for the first time. It scratched one of its tusks with its front claw. 'You look . . . odd.'

I nodded. 'I . . . I . . . I am dressed up for the big show later. I'm one of the actors. I'm meant to look funny. It's a comedy.'

The moon bug stared at me for a long moment. 'How delightful! You must be very talented. I hear over a thousand of us auditioned for that show! Good luck!'

I let out a small sigh of relief. And then an idea struck me. I had made a friend, so I might as well make use of them. 'Any chance you know where the queen is?'

I asked. 'I've got a message for her!'

The moon bug stared at me again for a moment and then laughed so hard it fell over on to its back with a loud *thwack* as it continued to laugh and roll around on its shell.

'Oh, you are so funny! I bet you're going to be great in this comedy show.' It let out another laugh. 'A message for the queen! How ridiculous! You know she is very royally busy. What a funny joke.' It chuckled a few more times before standing back up. 'Thank you for cheering me up. Now, no time to waste. We've got a whole city to finish building!' And with that, it flew off.

How would I ever convince the queen that she needed to forgive Spaceman Jack if I couldn't even find her? And the things here were worse than I realised. The moon

bugs had obviously been in here for a
LONG time if they had been able to create
an entire city! No wonder TUBS had been
acting funny. I thought about when I'd
first joined the crew and TUBS had crash-
landed unexpectedly on the babbit planet
and Captain Jane had fixed it. What if the
problem had been bigger even then? What
if the moon bugs had caused that problem
too?

It was more than an infestation! It was a
complete takeover!

The moon bugs snuck in and started
building the city without TUBS realising,
and then they must have reprogrammed
TUBS to listen to them . . .

Wait! That was it! The best idea was
there RIGHT in front of me!

I was a moon bug! If TUBS had been

reprogrammed to listen
to moon bugs, then
TUBS would listen to
me now. It already had
listened to me when it let

me in. As a moon bug, I would
be able to reprogramme TUBS back to its
own self.

I knew a little bit about programming
from my inventions. It was basically like a
set of rules for a computer. Programming
something like a spaceship would take
years and years of studying. And I didn't
have years to save TUBS.

But I did have a trick up my sleeve.

Or . . . a smart pellet in my pocket!

The smart pellet would tell me how
I could reprogramme TUBS! I just had to
hope that it was still somewhere on me,

since I wasn't in my spacesuit any more.

Aha! I had a little storage pocket, sort of like a kangaroo pouch, under my left wing! And there inside were the two smart pellets. Smaller than before, but still there.

All I had to do was find TUBS' CPU, or Central Processing Unit, which is basically computer speak for a machine's brain. (Human brains are sort of like the same thing as a CPU!) Then I had to swallow a smart pellet so I would know how to reprogramme it, and get to work! It was a perfect plan!

I leaned against the nearest wall and knocked. 'TUBS! It's me, Su– I mean, me! A moon bug! Please tell me where your CPU is.'

One of the wires beneath me lit up and

started flashing a bright orange. I smiled.
'Thank you, TUBS.'

I followed the wire through the walls
and deeper into the spaceship. The moon
bugs really had been very busy since taking
over. They had constructed an entire town!
Dozens of moon bugs were swimming and
sloshing in a pot from the canteen that
was strung up to the ceiling and filled with
water to make a pool.

There was a room with dozens of them

sitting around upturned bowls like they were tables, playing card games. I was pretty sure they were playing shoo-bop! I even saw the mini theatre they had made with seats and a stage and a digital screen that displayed the text: **Next show in 2 hours. Bring your own snacks! DO NOT EAT THE SEATS!**

The flashing wire seemed to go on forever until, finally, I saw it. The CPU. TUBS' brain. Hidden deep inside the spaceship, right beneath the control room.

The CPU was a pulsing and flashing hub. It looked a little bit like a human brain, but made of wires all tangled together. And in the middle was a keyboard where I knew I could type out commands.

I swallowed the smart pellet and thought as hard as I could *Reprogramme TUBS!*

And my brain went into SUPERPOWER
MODE! All of a sudden I knew exactly how
to reprogramme TUBS.

*Disconnect this wire, connect this one,
wait, that blue wire needs to be untied,
and now this one needs to be cut in half,
no scissors, must chew through it using my
moon-bug jaws, yum that is delicious, wait,
focus focus focus – I will be out of time
soon, OK, now to the keyboard,*

I need to use the computer code to reset TUBS – type type type – one more wire to reconnect and . . .

TUBS rumbled all around me and lights began flashing overhead.

'INTRUDER! INRUDER! INTRUDER!' shouted TUBS. **'CAPTAIN JANE! THERE IS AN INTRUDER IN MY BRAIN!'**

The smart pellet suddenly wore off and I was very aware that I was standing in the middle of a pile of wires, with a wire in my mouth. 'TUBS! It is ME! Suzie!'

The flashing lights dimmed for a moment. **'SUZIE?'** said the robotic voice. **'MY SENSORS TELL ME YOU ARE A MOON BUG. MOON BUGS TRICKED ME. MOON BUGS TOOK OVER. IS THIS ANOTHER TRICK?'**

'No! It is really me,' I said. 'Well,

technically I am a moon bug now. I turned into one so I could sneak back on to the ship and convince the queen to forgive Spaceman Jack. But then I couldn't find her, so I thought of an even better idea, which was to reprogramme you, and I did that . . .'

I knew I was babbling but I couldn't stop!

'HMMM,' said TUBS. **'THAT DOES SOUND LIKE SOMETHING YOU WOULD DO. AND I DO FEEL LIKE MYSELF. BUT I AM STILL FULL OF MOON BUGS! THEY ARE TICKLING MY INSIDES!'**

'Yes, about that,' I said. 'We need to figure out a way to get them out of you. I'm going to work on that next. I just need to find the queen!'

'LUCKY FOR YOU, I THINK SHE IS ON HER WAY HERE.'

CHAPTER 15

THE
QUEEN

'WHO DARES TO REPROGRAMME MY SHIP?'
A voice echoed all around me as something
burst through the wires.

I looked up and gasped. A sparkling moon
bug wearing a huge crown was flying towards
me, and she looked very, very angry.

It had to be Queen Moon Bug!

'You there! Small and strange-looking
moon bug! What are you doing!' she said to
me, gnashing her jaws in anger. 'Get out of
the control room! Royal access only!'

Before I could say anything, TUBS roared
to life. **'I AM NO LONGER YOUR SHIP! I
BELONG TO SPACE BLASTERS. I REPEAT,
I BELONG TO SPACE BLASTERS.'**

Queen Moon Bug gasped. 'You are MY
ship! I command you! I built an entire city
in your walls! I took you over from the
inside!'

**'AND NOW I AM MYSELF AGAIN.
REPROGRAMMED. BE GONE, QUEEN
MOON BUG.'**

'Where is the loyalty? You are a terrible spaceship! As terrible as that Spaceman Jack!' Queen Moon Bug was so mad she was shaking. She lifted a trembling leg and pointed at the control panel.

'If you are not loyal to me, I have no need for you, TUBS,' she sneered. 'MOON BUGS! TO ME! DEVOUR THE SHIP!'

'Wait!' I cried. There had to be a way for the moon bugs and the Space Blasters to live peacefully in the universe together. 'Stop!'

'MOVE, SMALL, STRANGE MOON BUG WHOM I DO NOT RECOGNISE, OR I WILL SQUISH YOU!' screeched Queen Moon Bug.

'I am not a moon bug!' I shouted. 'I am a human girl!'

'A HUMAN PRETENDING TO BE A MOON BUG?' Queen Moon Bug spat on the floor and unhinged her jaws. 'Humans are deceitful, terrible creatures! I should have known! You smelled wrong. I knew from the moment I flew into this control room and laid eyes on you that you were not one of my subjects.'

'Just give me a chance to explain,' I begged. More and more moon bugs were flying into the control room, drawn by their queen's shouting.

'Humans love to explain!' snarled the queen. 'They love to talk! They love to lie! NO! I have had enough of humans. Enough of creatures disrespecting me and my moon bugs! You'll be sorry. First, we will devour this ship! We will nibble every nail and bolt until there is nothing left. And then we will go from one planet to the next, until there is NOTHING LEFT. Nobody will laugh at us then! Or call us cheaters!'

Her moon-bug army cheered and
bared their teeth.

'But then there won't be anything
left,' I pointed out. 'And then what will
you do?'

'Then we will have the entire
universe to ourselves and it will be
peaceful.' Queen Moon Bug gave
me a fierce look, as if daring me
to disagree.

I bowed my head respectfully.
'Queen Moon Bug, I know what
happened with Spaceman
Jack,' I said. 'I know he

behaved VERY badly. And he deserves to be punished. But don't punish the entire universe just because of him! You are right – too many intergalactic creatures have underestimated you all. You are clearly amazing builders and inventors.' I gestured with a moon-bug arm. 'This city is incredible! You should be helping other aliens build their own cities. And then you can be paid to chew up their rubbish! Even in my short time as a moon bug, my jaws long to chew. Chewing space garbage is something moon bugs are good at, and are made for.

It is a skill that should be more respected. But it isn't the only thing you can do. There can be a new way forward. Don't just destroy everything. Build instead!' I raised my small moon-bug arms over my head in triumph. 'All hail the moon bugs, builders of the universe!'

'Do you think you can flatter me, and that is all it will take to keep us from destroying EVERYTHING?' said Queen Moon Bug. 'Because you know what I love even more than devouring things? COMPLIMENTS!' She flashed her sharp-toothed smile at me and I sighed in relief. It felt like my plan might just work!

'I know something you'll also like,' I said. 'A real apology from Spaceman Jack. And your shoo-bop cards back.'

Queen Moon Bug's smile disappeared.

'That human cannot be trusted.'

'Give him a chance to make it up to you and the rest of the moon bugs,' I pleaded. 'Wouldn't you rather be known as the beloved builders of the universe, and have all the space rubbish you want to eat, than the destroyers of it all?'

'I suppose when you put it like that . . .' The queen paused. 'What did you say your name was, strange human pretending to be a moon bug?'

I grinned at her, and felt my sharp moon-bug teeth poke out. 'I'm Suzie Wen. Human girl, inventor, member of Space Blasters, and friend to the moon bugs.'

CHAPTER 16

SHOO-BOP IN THE STARS

After I'd convinced Queen Moon Bug NOT to devour the entire universe, it was also easy to convince TUBS to forgive the moon bugs for secretly building a city in its walls and taking over its command centre.

'I NEED NEW SECURITY,' announced TUBS.

'You know,' said the yellow and green moon bug I'd replicated. 'I could stay a while on the ship. Show you how to protect yourself against future infestations.'

'HMMM,' TUBS thought. 'THAT MIGHT WORK.'

'That is a great idea!' I said. 'What did you say your name was?'

The yellow and green moon bug blinked at me with its huge eyes. 'Moon bugs don't have names. We have numbers. I'm moon bug number 793,865,542.'

'That takes way too long to say,' I said. 'What if I need to get your attention in a hurry? I know! How about we call you Seven? You'll fit right in, you know. We already have a Five-Eyed Frank, and a Three-Headed Tommy! So a Seven is perfect.'

'Seven,' the moon bug repeated.

'I like it!'

'Perfect,' I said with a grin. 'Now come on. Let's head outside the ship so you can meet everyone!'

At first, Five-Eyed Frank didn't like the idea of a moon bug joining the Space Blasters.

'Who gave you permission to add new members to the crew?' he said to me in a huff.

But after I explained that I'd not only convinced the moon bugs to not destroy TUBS, but also not to destroy the entire UNIVERSE, Frank admitted that maybe I might have a few good ideas. Including welcoming Seven to the Space Blasters.

And I was a *little* worried that Queen Moon Bug was going to attack Spaceman

Jack when she saw him, but she stayed calm. He, on the other hand, burst into tears and begged for forgiveness for being 'the weasel of the intergalactic card community' and called the head judge right then and there to ban himself forever from future tournaments, and to restore Queen Moon Bug's reputation.

Then he handed over the shoo-bop deck that he'd stolen from her.

'I know how we should seal our new deal,' the queen said with a big, toothy grin. 'A good old-fashioned shoo-bop game! Just between friends.'

'Wait!' I cried. 'Before we play shoo-bop, can someone turn me back into myself?'

'You got it,' said Five-Eyed Frank, bonking me on my moon-bug head three times.

And then I was back in my own body, wearing my spacesuit and everything!

Queen Moon Bug, who was now way smaller than me, looked me up and down. 'You looked better as a moon bug,' she said. 'But I suppose for a human, you aren't too bad. Now! Let's play shoo-bop!'

After we had played rounds and rounds of shoo-bop, it was time to say goodbye to Planet Zorg. The replicators came out of the tall purple grass, and some turned themselves into moon bugs, and some replicated us again. Even the knowledge worms poked their heads out of the ground to say goodbye. I was pretty sure the one who had helped me winked at me. As we boarded TUBS and got ready for take-off, the moon bugs and replicators all waved us off.

I was glad we'd had to crash-land on Planet Zorg. I really felt like part of the crew now. And best of all, I'd had a bigger adventure than I'd ever imagined!

It wasn't time for me to go home yet,

though. My crew, and the universe, still needed me!

'We still need to follow that distress signal across the universe,' said Captain Jane as we all buckled into our space seats. 'When someone in the galaxy needs help, the Space Blasters are there!' She smiled at me. 'Right, Suzie?'

'Right!' I flung my hand up in the air. 'For the universe!'

And then we blasted off on another adventure in the stars.

Acknowledgements

We are over the moon to have the best team in the entire universe working on SPACE BLASTERS! There is a whole awesome crew of people to thank.

First, we'd like to thank Claire Wilson, our agent, for being the captain of our publishing career and never steering us wrong. We'd also like to thank Safae El-Ouahabi at RCW for her assistance and support.

We love working with everyone at our Earth headquarters, Farshore! We would especially like to thank our superstar editors Asmaa Isse and Lindsey Heaven.

We would also like to thank Aleena Hasan for her work on the book, and on the marketing and PR side, we are so appreciative to Ellie Bavester, Jas Bansal, Sarah Sleath, Rory Codd, Pippa Poole, and Olivia Carson.

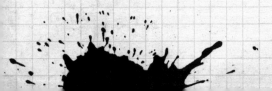

We'll be honest, our favourite part of SPACE BLASTERS are the incredible illustrations and amazing cover art! And for that we have to thank Ryan Hammond, the best designer in the universe, and the phenomenally talented illustrator Amy Nguyen. Thank you for bringing Suzie and the crew to life so perfectly. And the moon bugs are spectacular!

And huge thank you to the booksellers, librarians, and teachers who have introduced our books to young readers around the world! Special thanks to LJ Ireton at Waterstones Finchley Road and Sanchita Basu de Sarkar at the Children's Bookshop in Muswell Hill for their space-tacular support.

Of course, we have to thank our wonderful families! Thank you to our Tsang, Webber, Hopper, and Liu relatives all over Planet Earth.

Special thanks to Katie's siblings Jack and Jane for letting us steal their names. We also want to give a shout-out to Kevin's

sister Stephanie and our nephew Cooper who would always be welcome on the Space Blasters crew! We would also like to especially thank Kevin's parents, Louisa and Paulus AKA Lolly and Pop, for helping us watch our young daughters so we had time to write this book.

And to our daughters, who the book is dedicated to. Evie and Mira, you are our little explorers and make every day an adventure. We love you both so much.

KATIE AND KEVIN TSANG

Katie and Kevin Tsang are best-selling children's authors. They met in 2008 while studying at the Chinese University of Hong Kong. Since then they have lived on three different continents and travelled to over 40 countries together. In addition to the SPACE BLASTERS series, they are the co-authors of the young fiction series SAM WU IS NOT AFRAID and the DRAGON REALM books. Katie also writes YA as Katherine Webber. They currently live in London with their young daughters.